THE TALE OF THE PEAHEN

THE TORTOISE AND THE HANGMAN'S VOICE

ARYAN KAGANOF

HALF INCH PRESS

ISBN 978-1-969849-06-0

Although it's twenty years since I lost the peahen
she still haunts me and her words and aspirations still linger on
I owe nobody an apology for writing in English
yet inside me is this regret
that currently there is a handicap
that mars complete communication
between me and my audience,
particularly the peafowl audience

That the peahen had to run away
from home was preordained
You have been drinking, she whispered
Just a few beers, sweetheart, I responded
I'll carry you to bed, she said,
and I could not resist

I am still where she left me twenty years ago
she still haunts me and her scent
and her taste still linger on

I

For a long time, the peahen just stood
in the rubble of the factory, swaying
as if she did not know what to do
and did not know what to say

A day passed, however, then another, then a third —
she did not return, and I began to calm down
Then I saw the peahen walking
with steady steps, in a straight line

laughing between tears on the street
It wasn't the first time she had failed to make herself understood
And now here she stood and did not know what to do
and did not not know what to say

The reader is presented with a peahen
who is clearly a highly unconventional character
What is presented too, is a network of texts

representing the peahen's heritage of lovers
as it passes through the mind of the peahen
and out into the interview:

"Because I killed someone, a human male,
I could now be slain by anyone who meets me
When I returned to domestic life
I kept something to myself
I felt contempt for myself
and I ceased talking about those days."

But to get back to the beginning,
maybe "interview" is the wrong word
I do not see my peahen,
I hear her, but do not see her
Then I turn my head and look at the gun,
inches from my face
Although we usually die alone
the "interview" inevitably has a social dimension
But to get back to the beginning,
maybe "interview" is the wrong word

My peahen has this urge towards nature,
 an urge towards the open spaces
  I do not see my peahen,
   I hear her but do not see her
     Then I go to my room and lie on the bed and turn my head
and look at the gun, only inches from my face

And I may have had my reasons,
though you are not going to know them
But to get back to the beginning,
maybe "interview" is the wrong word

II

It has begun to be evening: into the sunless twilight
the piles of corpses stretch monstrously and threateningly
everything is expanded in them and everything expands
from them, in the dust that hangs in the air

Flickering candle lights begin to burn
and the air is stiflingly oppressive
with the stench of charnel

In the shell-gouged street the tortoise sees on every side,
in darkening windows, in reflections,
as if suddenly it is visible to him, a kind of chaos
            The human order

The further away from the main street, the fewer houses there are
The city boundary is a circular wall,
and outside that there is a desert in various tones of beige
Further away still there are dark-blue mountains,

or perhaps they are clouds, it is hard to tell
in the sunless twilight and anyway the tortoise
doesn't have time to study the far horizon
because just then the peahen appears on the street in front of him

Darling, she says to the tortoise, I know you've been going
through hell because I've been refusing to speak to you
His eyes follow her until she disappears in the shadows

She walks slowly until she reaches a huge pile of corpses
The world feels empty, she says, pointing with her beak
to the putrefacting mound of the dead, They've gone, you know
The tortoise looks up at the peahen with this weird sad little grin,

almost peaceful His lips move but no sound comes out
Suddenly he feels an urge to kiss her, mostly out of curiosity
to find out what a ghost's kiss feels like

I wasn't expecting that, is her comment afterward
Didn't you like it? the tortoise asks
But what do you think I am? Oh, you annoy me, the peahen says
You annoy me, you annoy me

What did you want to tell me? the tortoise asks
It is as if some last frontier dividing them has opened wide
The peahen's ghost feels a lustful softness and an ineffable
nearness,

a proximity less of the body than of the soul
It is as if she is gazing at herself out of the tortoise's eyes
and with every movement feeling
not only herself being touched by him

but also in some indescribable way
his sense of touching her —
it is a mysterious spiritual union

III

The tortoise began: Where was it you said you lived?
Why, I never did say, the peahen replied
Still, you must live somewhere
You ought to have a nice place, a fancy bird like you

Oh I have, the peahen said with enthusiasm
You have? The tortoise rolled his head around
in order to look at the peahen with increasing interest

     Consider for a moment: the tortoise as humble
and receptive supporting actor, as a sort of psychological slave
or confidant to the peahen The tortoise had wanted to run away
with the peahen, west, to California where they could live as man
and wife,

but she said We've lost enough time already
Look, said the young peahen, after resting for a moment,
I am enjoying this so far, and she showed the tortoise her stockings

Finish me, I beg you,
said the tortoise,
excited by the sight

As the tortoise straightened up he became aware of a new sound,
a repeated thudding that shook his shell, a thud that seemed to
come at three- or four-second intervals
He started to pace around

the hotel room as if he were too wound-up not to
Outside the missiles were landing
Are you all right? the peahen murmured more or less remotely,
as if she was thinking of him *somewhere else*

Huh? the tortoise said, No. Did I wake you up?
for he had thought she was asleep
You're better, the peahen announced, impressed,
as she flipped through the bouquets of flowers that had come

What will I do when I've been forgotten by all,
by all...? the tortoise hummed, What will I do
when I've been forgotten by all, by all...?

What's *all*?
The peahen swung behind him
into the elevator
I am finite, the tortoise said

But what about the time to come, the next stage
What comes *after* the present? the peahen asked
That would be the dream of fusing with the infinity
of the world, the tortoise declared, rather smugly

How can you help resenting the absurdity of time,
its march into the future, and all the nonsense about progress?
Why go forward, why live in time? the peahen asked,
sounding quite exasperated with the phlegmatic tortoise

I'm not guilty of having any choice in the matter, the tortoise said,
somewhat mystified by the peahen's train of questioning
As always she had only lied and smiled and tried to please him

Or so he thought
But now the elevator had arrived on the ground floor
The doors opened and the peahen ran laughing
through the hotel lobby into the night brightness,

between the roses and cosmos and Shasta daisies,
down the gravel path and beyond the heaps of grass
swept from the lawns
Wait for me, the tortoise complained,

as he cautiously threaded his way
after the peahen, along the half familiar path
She was throwing her voice into his mouth,
distorting it into a ventriloquist trick

"No dog is so evil that it does not wag its tail.
A dog who has been washed has been washed clean
without our aid in our absence."

Then suddenly, as though summoned upwards
by this uncanny incantation of the peahen's,
the earth rises towards the tortoise
I'm dead! he thought

But at the same moment he found himself seated
on some soft earth His nose touched some grass; he had fallen,
unharmed into the midst of a meadow

He does not cry because he is a tortoise who thinks constantly
about the peahen he loves and who is dead
but who died a long time ago
After she died,
the tortoise realised
that he had tuned into her way
of doing things, her way of thinking things,
that he had fitted something of his mental life to hers
and given himself over to the peahen with the confidence
of belonging to the unknown

Then there is a pause

A brief pause, or a very long pause,

depending on the kind of aptitude the good reader has for patience

IV

The sky darkens now as they enter the desert
Where would you like to eat? the tortoise says
and the peahen's ghost giggles, I don't eat anymore
Obviously this is not a typical love story

        One may say
that in an occupied territory there is no *typical* life at all
The sun was up now as the tortoise and the peahen's ghost
crossed over to the far edge of the desert

Who are you? the tortoise says, What should I call you?
What's your name? . . .
But she no longer seems to hear him
She has brought him here

in order for him to accept
what all of us must accept one day

The tortoise knows what to do with his body
He remembers

You approach death with a clear mind
You choose the right place

Now the tortoise speaks to the good reader from beyond the grave

I'm going to repeat myself a little, can't be helped . . . just a few
things to say about the peahen . . .
she is a lot like me — we've both of us
felt the force of a love throughout our entire lives

Not necessarily a love already in existence, but something

that wasn't there yet, that was going to come — or to end
That's part of why this story was written:
to produce that irreducible
final moment, about which nothing more needs to be said

From across the far side of the desert the sky lights up
as a fresh set of missiles rain down on the city
The tortoise would cry if he could but all of his tears
have been shed

What is left for his body
to do is crumble

He joins the peahen thinking
now at last
I know where she lives

V

The peahen walked because it gave her the illusion of change
Of a future
The city reeked of heat and longing
Everything fermented
The corner shop was selling eggs
stacked like skulls and Coke in sweating bottles
She bought a box of cigarettes,
and stood outside the spaza shop, unable to open the packet
with her beak, tasting not the tobacco but the memory of the
hangman's voice

He used to light her cigarettes
A hand, a match, a shared ember
They'd smoked in sync,
each drag an act of tenderness

At first the silence between them
had been warm, a secret held in breath
But over time it became armour
Sometimes she fantasized about walking
out of the city, past the edge of maps

He was drunk Laughing too loud Hands too big Face distorted
She realized: he would crush her
Not with fists
But with his indifference
The breakup wasn't dramatic
He said, We're moving in together — meaning her replacement,
the other bird
She remembered nodding, Saying O
That's how loss sounded, like nothing

Now she wandered through streets she didn't recognize
Claws wet Feathers glued to her temples
Buildings leaned over her like questions

She saw him again by accident

He was outside a café She stopped, frozen
Her body surged with tension
He waved Too casually Too unlike him
Then his other bird arrived

A crested quetzal
with a long flowing train of tail feathers
Nacreous Beautiful

The peahen turned away, fast
The pavement turned too
Light shattered on tar
She walked without direction,
the peahen who walks too quickly,
who looks like she's fleeing or arriving
That night she dreamed of him
Or maybe she didn't sleep It didn't matter

    Abandoned
Flaking
But still standing
inside me Nothing

    You gone
check phone
less than silence My eyes

    like bruises Inside: Nothing
deeper than fear

close eyes
instinct as alarm,
I want to forget how your mouth met my eyes

     How Nothing
sleeps now
static pulse, phone
ringing bed

lit cigarette Nothing
breathing eyes
it's not fear —

it's form A thickening I birthed Nothing
on a night you forgot me Now phone
buzzing blink shadow

behind eyes,
in me, shadow
beckons Fear
I wanted to strangle Nothing (gently)

Now I live with Nothing
eyes open
body all shadow (Ashes)

VI

She walks around, touching what was his,
tongue warm, body soft
vinyl spins, needle drops

She walks around, touching what was his
she spreads her legs, remembers the kiss —
différance dissolved
vinyl spins, needle drops

Face between thighs
"take your top off,"
she walks around, touching what was his

She wings the abyss
the smell of him still there
vinyl spins, needle drops

She bites the hand that feeds her She doesn't care
she walks around, touching what was his
vinyl spins, needle drops

She stomps pounds — just feet, no sound
alone at night She doesn't care
She runs, flies, burns,
doesn't care

Her skirt is up Her mouth tastes metallic air
A key clenched hard — no memory, no ground
The ocean whispers How many ghosts swim there?

She vomits up stars above the sea, spell broken
She walks barefoot, alone at night She doesn't care
Everything is cheap, each individual incredulous object so stark

15

A suitcase open, memory unclean

She sits in silence, fingers numb
scrolls his name, deletes it in the dark
The words — *I love you* — wiped clean
différance dissolved

VII

You will never affect me again
This life and death belong to me
I am beyond your shadowed grasp

I tried to meet you where you had reigned,
But found no echo, no buried key
You will never affect me again

What I revealed, you soiled for sport
Laughed at the soul I gave for free
I am beyond your shadowed hold

Your new bird mimics all I was, and then
Tries wearing me like finery
But you will never affect me again

Her halo glows with cheap scent
    Selah! Amen!
But none of that can touch what we —
I am beyond your shadowed grasp

Scatter, spoil, destroy, pretend
Still, I refuse your jewelled cruelty
You will never affect me again
I am beyond your shadowed hold

VIIII

Time in Mountain

Mountains hold deep time
Not clock-time, but geologic time
folded, pressed, enduring
Time in mountain is not movement, it is weight
It is the archive of planetary memory
Erosion is the mountain *thinking* Avalanche is its sentence.
Time in mountain is duration that watches you back

Time in Fire

Here time is not stable
Fire devours time
Fire is speed, destruction, and alchemy
Time in fire is a threshold, a *becoming*
Not endurance, but transformation
The past is burned, the future is released as smoke
Time in fire is what cannot return the same

Time in Forest

Time in forest is neither linear nor still
It breathes It decays It returns
Here, time is layered
fungi digesting memory,
roots curling through the residue of ancestors,
branches catching the light of forgotten mornings

Time in forest is not marked by seconds
but by the soft violence of rot,
by the slow patience of lichen,
by the ghosts of deer paths fading under moss

It is peripheral time
the kind that notices you only when you stop speaking

It is the opposite of clock
It is being watched by a thousand eyes that don't blink,
who remember you not as a person,
but as a disturbance in the pattern of leaves

      Time in forest *listens*

It is neither origin nor destination
but ambient presence
the lull between death and renewal,
the green pause where the world
remakes itself without asking

or being asked

IX

The policeman slammed the door on the peahen
with a bang that reverberated inside the whole cell block
For some time the peahen could not fully grasp her change of
circumstances
Everything had happened so quickly and so unexpectedly
the blinding lights, the barking voice,
the triumphant shout of the policeman

To her own confusion, the peahen collapsed
in a heap on the ground,
buried her face in her wings
and began to weep and rock herself rhythmically

Then, looking at the silence
The peahen knew the answer
The only thing she had valued in life
had been taken from her

After a while, it came to the peahen to pawn herself for money

X

The fire in the centre of the ruins blazes
bright enough to light up the car-park
She tells herself that she is happy
Because here, in the centre, there is a chance

Two men are sitting cross-legged, broiling
chunks of meat on sticks over the coals
The fire in the centre of the ruins blazes bright
She tells herself that she is happy

She's never killed anyone but now she's going to
She begins to laugh louder and louder, until
the whole car-park rings with pealing echoes
In all her life she has never been free

She reaches into her bosom
pulls out a small piece of paper
Goodbye, goodbye! I kiss you
and love you, she says

She begins nodding her head
and pointing her wing at the sky
In the middle of the car-park
there are children at play building a snowman
She turns around and faces the crematorium
She reaches into her bosom
pulls out a small snub nosed revolver
Goodbye, goodbye! I kiss you
and love you, she says

Darkness is kept at bay by the fire in the centre of the ruins
For an hour they exchanged places,
wandering silently around the dusty room,
stretching their arms out to feel its unconfined emptiness,
grasping at the sensation of absolute spatial freedom

The hangman walked toward the back of the crematorium
The peahen followed him in silence
Dusk had settled, and the embers of the fire glowed in the darkness
She fell asleep then, her head against his chest,
unaware that a new white sun had risen

XII

A transformation is taking place
in the sky and on the earth
This isn't junk and ashes   This is our life
And so, as I am looking at the sky,
the peahen suddenly seizes me by the elbow
And I realise the impossibility
which love comes up against

The peahen's eyes bulged bulged bulged
At five in the afternoon we saw
several armed soldiers standing in the car-park
Her eyes bulged bulged bulged
        What did I do to deserve this? Am I a killer?
Her eyes bulged bulged bulged

Freedom is indeed a priceless gift
The old life rewrites itself every minute
But she did not have long to wait
The sea began to vibrate
with waves that spread out in a circle
She isn't sad or depressed
She is saved from all that

by the sun coming in the windows
illuminating objects with brilliant light
The old life rewrites itself every minute

The most terrible thing was the realization
that what had happened was irreversible

The old life rewrites itself every minute
Freedom is indeed a priceless gift

23

XIII

That night the peahen slept on a low, straw bed
in the same room as the hangman

It was soon evident that the hangman
had an aptitude, a remarkable gift

The peahen made the observation
that the hangman's existence

is fundamentally on two planes:
    cowardice is horribly infectious
    but courage can be infectious too

The peahen and the hangman
exchanged some experiences
they'd had in their common hometown,
named a whole series
of names they both knew,
laughed a few times,
and the peahen noticed
the hangman even guffawed once

Did he know he was about to die?

XIV

No choice is possible

The hangman speaks in a loud voice,
(but not too loud)
distinctly so everybody can hear him

No choice is possible

The hangman not only
didn't master his existence
but was destroyed by it

The hangman is characterized
by the narrowness
of his obsessive repetitions
and on the other hand
by an astonishing freedom of choice, that is:

No choice is possible

Now the hangman arises with a slight bow
and pushes back his chair

The hangman moves in closer and cradles
the peahen's cheek, causing a noise to escape

her beak when he deepens the kiss, thanking her
for this beautiful life that's given him these grey hairs

I drank half the glass and then I felt very giddy
I lay down
As long as I kept my eyes open it wasn't so bad

25

The hangman said, You ought to take your feathers off
His face seemed enormous

      The next day the hangman and I walked all afternoon
      in a pale sunlight without any warmth
The hangman's eyes were haggard
tortured by jealousy, burnt up by longing

      Had I really *done* that? Kissed him *there*?

XV

The peahen set off for the shops as usual
A good distance away, there stood a baobab tree
The baobab tree asked the peahen her life story
So the peahen did not go to the shops
Rather she stood in the shade that the enormous baobab tree
offered
and told her story:
  I refused to do the dirty work
  Choose some other bird, I said
  But the Hangman roared: Let debt make the peahen suffer
  so that she'll be sorry she refused the dirty work
  Then I saw death near
  I was looking at the sky thinking of my death
  The Judge said I must sit down
  When the jury saw me sit, there was excitement all over
  The crows shouted "Hoo-o-o-o!"

The baobab tree waved goodbye and the peahen continued to the
sparkling shops
Maybe I am lost in the shadow of life, the peahen said
This sweet shadow which beneath the surface
and the mask
makes things visible
and describable

 In any case, I do not want to speak
about shadows
my shadow has lost that ridiculous freedom
   I still possess
it is no longer she
who chooses not to leave

XVI

The peahen was wearing a little knitted cap
far too small for her
from which wisps of turqoise feathers were sticking

The illuminated letters above our heads
began to flicker a warning, and a voice from concealed
loudspeakers advised us to fasten our seatbelts
and prepare for the landing

Then we both knelt and prayed together

From that day on, the peahen never knew starvation

Today, as I splash my head in cold water
I distantly remember the peahen suggesting
separate sleeping corners for the nights

XVII

In the peahen's universe
every fragment
is a luminous detail

Thrust into the apocalyptic
turmoil of our car-park
the peahen must have felt the earth
trembling beneath her claws

    The analysis carried out here,
of necessity cursory and summary,
is sufficient proof, all the same,
that any sort of scientific un-
derstanding of the essence
of the peahen is attainable
only in the degree to which
we resolve the fundamental prin-
cipled and methodological problems
which a study of this peahen places before contemporary readers.

In the peahen's universe every fragment is a luminous detail

XVIII

Suddenly the peahen feels like singing
We are nothing, my friend
we know nothing, she sings

    And song, which has delivered her,
is an abstract function
and an *a priori* power
of peahen nature,
it is the movement
whereby at every moment
the peahen frees herself from history,
                in short, it is the exercise of freedom

Again the peahen sings *"We are nothing,*
my friend, we know nothing."

XIX

The peahen delicately cleared her throat,
Have you made me your project?
The hangman shivered with delight
The peahen stared at him, fascinated

On the whole, it is all rubbish, your going to a farm, the hangman
said
It is the "it", the now, the word that the hangman wanted

Shadows are like ink in the white sunlight
I am a little frightened now that I am coming to my senses
And so I have adopted a radical new approach

to the peahen

The peahen understands nothing of what goes on around her
Gargantuan forces, both political and aesthetic,
that have been held in some relationship
of opposition or tension within and around her expansive body,
finally dissolve
in one last aporetic image: her madly laughing in the car-park
shadows,
    like ink
in the white sunlight

At the end of the rainbow
the peahen hears a Voice
                I'm a student, you see
I'm making a study of monuments

The peahen and the Hangman's Voice now take
                          their first few dancing steps

Yes, the best way the peahen and the Hangman's Voice
can serve the revolution
is to dance as well as they are able
                              the tarantella
              even the fandango

XX

For a full twenty-four hours the tortoise
told me about his relationship with the peahen
Through that narration I came face to face
with my rival
Throughout his story I kept quiet
Inside I was wincing

     Love is a war zone
In some room, in some building, in some street,
I came face to face with my rival
For a full twenty-four hours I matched the tortoise's
                    wordiness
word for word
with my silence

We then found ourselves taking an intense dislike to each other
As to be expected
when I got home
and purged the claus-
trophobic smell
of stale blood
from my skin
I knew the peahen
and I were finished

XXI

It has become clear to me
that although the peahen feels the same way
about the situation as I do,
there are enormous, perhaps insurmountable
differences between us

Ah, she said in her peculiar way
Would you like to come inside?
I followed her into the small, dimly lit nest
with its raised bed, carefully made, and piled high
with white linen

Look, my dear, I said to the peahen,
we are not going to stay here
I can't live in a place like this

Is this... what education has done to you? the peahen asked angrily
Her gold earrings swung as she leaned forward
I soon forgot everything
and did what she was doing

But the next morning we both realised
there was no money and hence no breakfast
therefore the peahen despatched me

It did not take me long
to reach the crematorium
where I hoped to find
gainful employment

XXII

I remember my first minor collison
in a deserted hotel car-park
I sat quietly, sometimes turning my head

        Open your eyes, open your eyes
Three or four human shapes watch
from the edge of the car-park
I open my eyes as the clouds overhead
                                start to coalesce
                                and the sky takes on
                                its regular weight

I could see the empty keyhole,
but I couldn't hear a sound
I then looked at the rifle in my lap
and had a feeling that I would soon
be using it (The injunction to act now)

Back home at the radar station, I carefully washed
my hands with soap, did the same to my face,
then sat down on the floor and watched the day
transition into hyperstasis No particles, no fields,
                        just endless groove

A knock at the front door What the hell,
nobody knows I'm holed up here When I open the door,
pinch-faced, exhausted, a peahen stands before me
Help me, I have only one life and that life is trickling
towards death, the peahen says

Surprised that the peahen can talk,
Shall we go to my office, I say

I started down the steps
The peahen looked quickly behind her,
then followed Once inside my office

I gestured to the peahen to take a seat
and sat down myself opposite her
What are your intentions as regards me? the peahen asked,
nervously,
her eyes darting around my office

It took me a long time to realize that what counts
is not your intention but what you actually achieve, I said

Do you know why I have come? the peahen asked

Yes, I said
So that you will never part from me again

XXIII

The years, as they say, passed
But these notes are not intended to be about myself
but about the mysterious peahen, about whom
I have again thought very often and very intensively
during the past few days, and perhaps I shall succeed now,

after a number of unsuccessful attempts along those lines,
in putting these recollections down on paper
The peahen had names
I had my own names
She had variations of names
I had forged documents
Obviously it was a complicated affair

Not to mention the problem of inter-species communication
At first I couldn't understand much of what she said,
maybe because I had changed position
or because she was speaking more softly

I turned over
She said she had lost something important and she wanted to die,
that was all
And then suddenly I was fighting with the peahen
I broke loose
She grabbed me again with her wings
What a battle! What a ruckus!

I couldn't disentangle myself
The noise was awful
She had me in a drowning-man's grip
She was cracking my head with her questions

But suppose my eyes aren't blue enough? she said
Blue enough for what?
I want I want to capture I want to possess
Did she mean me? But I was hers
Surely she understood that?

XXIV

Actually the peahen understood nothing about me
But it took me a long time to realise that
Possibly just as long as it took her to realise
that I understood nothing of her
                              Have I already mentioned that inter-
                                    species
                                    relationships are not easy?

When the iron door finally closed behind us,
the peahen drew in a long breath to let out a howl,
but she remembered that I was still there,
and all I heard was a deep almost human sigh

Then she proudly closed her eys and settled down for the night
The next morning the peahen gave me an inviting look
But at the time I only had eyes for her shadow
How beautiful she is on the wall! Just as I like her to be
I sat down to compare the one with the other

Confused by my divided attention, the peahen arched herself,
thrusting out her chest and her hips, but the shadow was better
at that game than the peahen was
Then I feebly reproached myself
for my inclination to love in the peahen some colourless image of
her on the wall

What's wrong with you? she asked me
I really didn't know   Thinking I could keep her
was crazy in the first place

Within the fever of her restlessness
the peahen was losing her bird shape

39

She was delimiting the horizons,
sinking into planets without axis,
losing her polarity
and the divine knowledge of fusion

While I was hatching rebellious thoughts, the peahen
regained
her self-control
Exceedingly calm now, she addressed me in a precise voice:
Oh, anguish and despair!
And when all her gestures and talk seemed lulled,
suddenly she sprang up again
with a new mood and a nervous lithe walk,
while she churned ideas like leaves on a pyre
which never turned to ash

XXV

It was already past midnight
Now the peahen had run out of hiding places
She fell silent and assumed a greedy expression,
drawing a vague sketch
in the air with her beak
Later the rise of the global economy
would create fierce competition between the species,
which swept away all the dreams of integrating
the various animal populations
into a vast pseudo-human class
with ever-rising incomes
Whole animal genuses fell through the net
and joined the ranks of the feral wildings

But the savage sexual competition
did not abate as a result—quite the reverse
Nonetheless when there is love, there is no death;
there is death only when the thought process arises

When there is love, there is no death,
because there is no fear
and love is not a continuous state
Love is merely being from moment
to moment
Therefore, love is condemned to its own eternity

The few days I spent in the company of the peahen
were the sum total of my worthwhile days on this earth
When she tried to fly away I wrang her neck
cut her throat

41

and bled her

Once she quit flopping
around I plopped her body
into a basin of near boiling water
The hot water loosened up the skin so I could pluck
the beautiful grey and turqouise feathers more easily

I singed the hair of the skin by rotating the body
over newspaper lit on the barbecue, scrubbed the skin
well and then opened the back of the peahen, extracted the guts
Roasted and ate her

Back home at the radar station,
I carefully washed my hands with soap,
did the same to my face, sat down on the floor
and watched the day transition into hyperstasis.

XXVI

43

I do not remember exactly when
or in what circumstances I left the crematorium

My feelings were confused about it
I had a very blurry memory of the crematorium

before I decided to rescue it piece by piece
from the memory of others

In the crematorium I have left behind, the failure
has been complete My life, in my own hands

My actions But I am unable to run away from the crematorium,
for me everything is possible, except life...

XXVII

After I left the crematorium
I shook and shook
and saw the most powerful visions,
and the sharpest colours,
and the strangest shapes,
and I wasn't sure where I was
My eyes were sad in joy sometimes

Moving my head
up and down ruefully,
I paid no attention to the potholes in the road
A heavy storm was coming up,
and I stood still
to conserve my energies
and to gaze with wonderment
at the emerald meadowland
opposite the crematorium

Half a mile from the crematorium
I could hear the sea
washing on the beaches
through the darkness,
the onshore winds whipping
at the crests of the dunes in the moonlight

I am now nothing more than an eye
And lifting my eyes, red-hot with sleeplessness,
to the sky, I shout out a speech about the dead birds
of the crematorium, about this proud phalanx pounding
the anvil of future centuries
with the hammer of history

I have reached that stage of life when one can't help wondering
who's next, but I rarely linger on the topic of death
for there is nothing more execrable
than existence *after* the crematorium.

XXVIII

Dear Friend,
may I have a minute of your time?
What I would like for us to do
is to introduce the crematorium
at the centre of our eroded faith
in what were once our core beliefs

It was a magnificent and terrible sight,
to see the humans march on to the tune of their flutes,
without any disorder in their ranks, any discompsure
in their minds or change in their countenances,
calmly and cheerfully moving with music into the ovens

It is not every species that can meditate its own ruin,
not every society that can imagine its own decay
A surveillance camera has been set up for the occasion
near the front row of the crematorium

Whatever my feelings at the time of leaving it,
I know that I shall one day return to the crematorium
Everything happens as is anticipated
my poem is finished.

Aryan Kaganof is editor and publisher of the South African cultural archive herri (https://herri.org.za/12). Portions of this poem have appeared in *Home Planet News* and *Best New African Poets 2025* (Mwanaka Media).